WALT DISNEY PRODUCTIONS
presents

SINDBAD
and the
ROBBER BIRDS

Random House 🏠 **New York**

First American Edition. Copyright © 1982 by Walt Disney Productions. All rights reserved under International and Pan-American Copyright Conventions. Published in the United States by Random House, Inc., New York, and simultaneously in Canada by Random House of Canada Limited, Toronto. Originally published in Denmark as SINDBAD OG DE MYSTISKE FUGLE by Gutenberghus Gruppen, Copenhagen. ISBN: 0-394-85483-7 Manufactured in the United States of America   2 3 4 5 6 7 8 9 0
A B C D E F G H I J K

Sindbad the Sailor had been on a long trip.
Now at last he was ready to sail home.

He had a large chest of jewels to sell in
his home market.

And he had found a place on a sailing ship
that was loading at the docks.

Sindbad boarded the ship and went to
his cabin.

He took a last look at his jewels.

Then he locked the jewel chest and
stored it in the hold.

Sindbad went up on deck again.

He watched other traders come aboard with their goods.

He saw ivory tusks and bundles of furs.

There were barrels and boxes and crates and jars.

Just as the gangplank was being pulled up,
one last trader dashed on board.
He held a large bundle with care.

"I have mirrors here," the trader told
the captain. "Fine looking glasses for ladies.
Very breakable! I must keep them with me!"

Sindbad greeted his cabin mates—
the mirror seller and two other traders.
The mirrors stayed in the cabin too.

"Cast off!" ordered the captain,
and the ship set sail.

For many days the weather was fine.
The traders stayed on deck and told tales
of their travels.

Sindbad became good friends with
his cabin mates.
One man sold silk and one sold honey.
The third man was the mirror seller.

One afternoon black clouds rolled in.

"Uh-oh!" said the man with the mirrors.

"Get ready for a hard blow!"

The mirror seller was right.
By nightfall the ship was tossing
in a fearful storm.

The traders listened with alarm
to the sounds of crashing from the hold.
The mirror seller held on to his bundle.

Suddenly the ship rolled so hard that
the mirror seller flew out of bed.

He landed on his bundle of mirrors.

CRUNCH! went the mirrors.

"Oy, I am ruined!"
the mirror seller
cried.

By morning the storm was over, and
the traders went down to the hold.

What a mess!

Chests and jars had broken open.

Honey had spilled all over the bolts of silk and Sindbad's jewels.

"I am ruined!" cried the seller of silks.

"So am I!" cried the honey trader.

"My chest is ruined," said Sindbad.
"But my jewels can not be hurt by honey.
Help me clean them, and I will try
to help you."

Sindbad carried
his broken chest
and sticky jewels
up to the deck.
"Bring up some silk
and broken honey jars,"
he told his friends.

Sindbad borrowed a bucket and
hauled up sea water with it.

Then he and his friends washed
the sticky silk.

Next they washed the jewels in jars
and spread them on the silk to dry.

That night the four friends slept on deck
to guard the jewels.

When the moon rose, the jewels sparkled
in its light.

A flock of birds flew by the ship.
These birds liked shiny things.
When they saw the jewels, the birds
flew down and scooped them up!

All the jewels were gone when Sindbad
awoke in the morning.

"My jewels!" he cried. "Where are they?"

"Look!" said the mirror seller.
"There are marks on the silk.
These are the prints of birds' feet!"

"Robber birds!" said
the honey trader.
"They steal anything
that shines!"

Sindbad climbed up to
the crow's-nest and looked
through a spyglass.

"I see an island," he said.
"Birds are flying around
a big tree. Robber birds!"

"I must go ashore," said Sindbad.
"I must get back my jewels."
"We will help you," said his friends.

"I see a way to rescue my jewels,"
said Sindbad. "I will need to use
the ruined silk and broken mirrors."
"Help yourself," said the traders.

"May I use your rowboat?" Sindbad asked
the captain, and the captain agreed.

Finally all was ready.

The traders got into the boat, and it was lowered to the water.

They rowed and rowed until they came to the island.

Sindbad pulled out a bag of broken mirrors. He scattered the pieces along the beach.

Then Sindbad led the way to
the robber birds' big tree.
The birds slept there every night.
The traders waited until dark.

Then the traders began to shout
and hit the tree with sticks.
The noise frightened the birds away.

Away flew the birds, away over the beach.

The birds saw the bits of mirror
shining in the moonlight.
They flew down and picked them up.

Hidden by the dark, the traders climbed
to the robber birds' nests.
There they found Sindbad's jewels!
They quickly gathered them up.

The traders put the jewels into bags
made from the ruined silk.

Then they raced to the shore and
at dawn returned to their ship.

When the traders were safely on board,
the captain called out orders to his crew.
Up came the anchor, and the ship set sail.

The traders went into their cabin.
Sindbad divided his jewels into
four equal piles—one for each of them.
"You helped me," Sindbad said to
his friends, "and now I will help you."